Text and illustrations copyright © 2016 by Ashley Spires

Tundra Books, a division of Random House of Canada Limited, a Penguin Random House Company

Library and Archives Canada Cataloguing in Publication

Spires, Ashley, 1978-, author, illustrator
      Over-scheduled Andrew / by Ashley Spires.

Issued in print and electronic formats.
ISBN 978-1-77049-484-8 (bound).–ISBN 978-1-77049-485-5 (epub)

      I. Title.

PS8637.P57O94 2016   jC813'.6   C2015-901068-3
                                                 C2015-901069-1

Published simultaneously in the United States of America by Tundra Books of Northern New York, a division of Random House of Canada Limited, a Penguin Random House Company

Library of Congress Control Number: 2015931507

Edited by Tara Walker
Designed by Kelly Hill
The artwork in this book was rendered digitally and with a great deal of over-scheduling.
The text was set in Neutraface.

Printed and bound in China

www.penguinrandomhouse.ca

1   2   3   4   5   20   19   18   17   16

TUNDRA BOOKS | Penguin Random House

OVER-SCHEDULED Andrew

written and illustrated by Ashley Spires

Tundra Books

Andrew loved putting on plays. He joined the drama club so he could wear costumes and perform on a real stage.

His best friend Edie helped him learn his lines on the way home from school.

Sometimes they got a little distracted.

Andrew was a natural actor, but even naturals have to practice. His teacher suggested that he work on his public speaking by joining the debate club.

As Andrew's voice got stronger, so did his arguments.

He won so many of his debates that Calvin suggested he use his smarts for chess club.

Three clubs seemed like a lot, but Andrew could manage.

During play rehearsals, Andrew found it hard to keep up with the dance routines.

So he signed up for ballet lessons and a karate class to improve his coordination.

A ndrew was busy. Three days a week he stayed after school for one of his clubs.

Afterwards, he went to ballet or karate then home for dinner, homework and bed.

He's very good.

But his new classes were helping with drama club. He spoke his lines clearly and loudly, and he danced gracefully.

And even with all his activities, Andrew made sure to see Edie.

There was always time for fun.

Until Coach asked Andrew to play for the tennis team.

And Chris begged him to be the school newspaper editor.

And Grandma insisted that he learn to play the bagpipes.

Andrew was busier and busier, and his days were longer and longer. To make matters worse, he kept finding things that he wanted to do.

He joined French film club to learn more about acting.

Au revoir, Papa!

He started singing lessons to help him hit the high notes.

Dónde está el baño?

And he signed up for Spanish classes because speaking another language is just plain useful.

At least Andrew still got to spend time with Edie — though only for fifteen minutes on Friday afternoons, between bagpipe lessons and French film club.

Unfortunately, he rarely stayed awake for the full fifteen minutes.

Keeping up with his schedule left Andrew exhausted. His tired eyes missed mistakes in the newspaper.

During singing lessons, his tone was flat.

Nuuugggg . . .

And his reflexes weren't quite what they used to be.

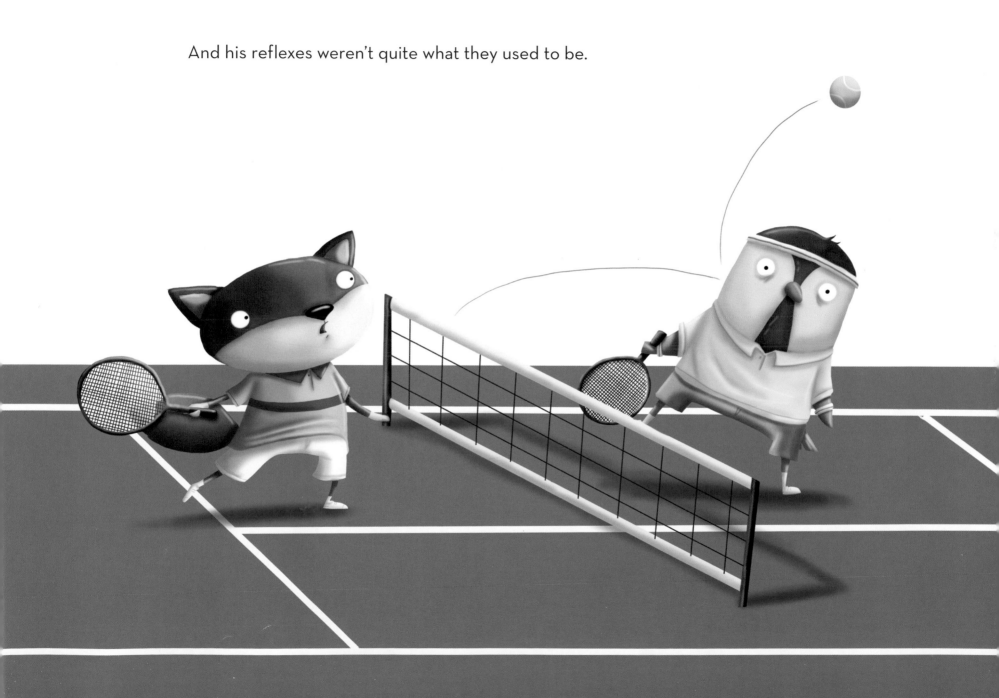

Andrew's schedule was getting all mixed up in his head.

He danced his way through debate club.

For example ...

He argued his way through karate.

He honked his way through tennis.

And he backhanded his chess match.

Worst of all, he missed his cue in the big drama club performance.

When Andrew woke up,
everyone had gone home.

Almost everyone.

All his hard work had been for the play, and he had missed the whole thing. Andrew had never been so sad. He felt just like a character in a French film.

Clearly, he was doing too much.

The next day Andrew quit debate, chess, ballet, karate, tennis, Spanish, the bagpipes and the newspaper.

He didn't quit everything though.

There was always another drama club performance.

Or French film to watch.

Now Andrew was free to walk home with Edie again and get distracted.

They even met up with some friends and formed a new club . . .

. . . the no-schedule kind!